Where Did My Happy Go?

Annie Penland

ISBN: Softcover   978-1-7960-4684-7
        Hardcover   978-1-7960-4685-4
        EBook   978-1-7960-4683-0

This is a work of fiction. All of the characters, names,
incidents, organizations, and dialogue in this novel are
either the products of the author's imagination or are
used fictitiously.

Print information available on the last page

Rev. date: 07/16/2019

To order additional copies of this book, contact:
Xlibris
1-888-795-4274
www.Xlibris.com
Orders@Xlibris.com

Where Did My Happy Go?

My Happy is a feeling that makes me smile and laugh. She likes bright colors and cheerful sounds. We play, explore and sometimes just hang around.

But now my Happy's gone! Where did she go? Has anyone seen her? Does anybody know?

Is she sad like me? Is she all alone? Does she know it's hard to have fun when your Happy is gone?

I remember playing with her and all the fun we had before...could she be waiting for me somewhere, wanting to play some more?

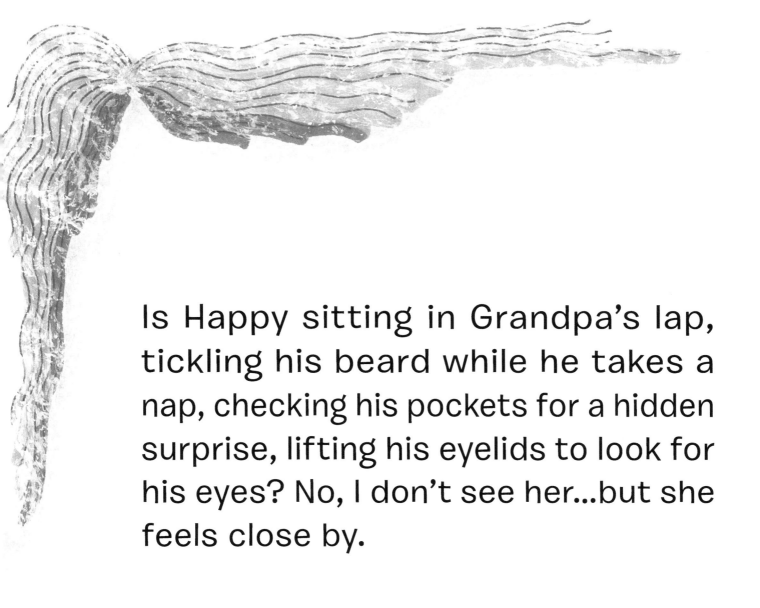

Is Happy sitting in Grandpa's lap, tickling his beard while he takes a nap, checking his pockets for a hidden surprise, lifting his eyelids to look for his eyes? No, I don't see her...but she feels close by.

Maybe Happy is eating strawberry pancakes, watching Mommy cook, or sitting in the living room window reading a dinosaur book? No, Happy isn't here... is she?

I usually have fun riding my bike, racing down the rolling, tumbling hills, going faster and faster, laughing harder and harder, bouncing up and down till I spill. Happy, I think I saw you at the top of the hill!

Is Happy watching the goldfish swimming around in the pond or ringing the garden chimes, BING BONG BING BONG BING BONG? Is she the one giving me happy feet that want to dance around?

The puppy's kisses tickle my nose and the kitty has soft, silky fur. I watch them play hide and seek with each other and bark and cuddle and purr. Look! The puppy's tail is wagging and the kitty is rolling in the sun. Happy! Are you helping them have fun?

How about going to the park? It's fun to swing way up high, way down low. I pump my legs back and forth as hard as I can go. Wow! Happy, I feel like a bird flying high above the world!

Look, a snail! I have so much fun with snails...watching them crawl, touching their shells, following their shiny, slimy snail trails. Happy, are you down in the cool, deep, green grass waiting for the hot afternoon sun to pass?

This mud puddle is great! I jump and splash and get all wet, mud getting everywhere that lovely squishy mud can get. Happy, I know you can't resist this!

It's time to take a bubble bath, soak in warm water, bathe in the tub, use animal sponges to wash and squeeze and scrub. Water and bubbles go everywhere... I hear Happy laughing!

Then come bedtime stories about giants and dinosaurs and kings and the happy, silly songs that Mommy sometimes sings. Being with Mommy always feels good. She says Happy lives inside us and wouldn't leave us if she could.

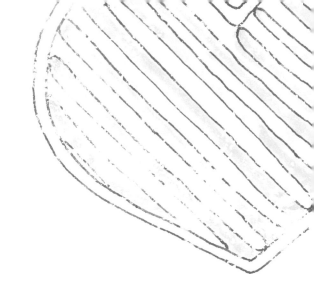

Now it's time for Mommy and Daddy's good night kisses and hugs. They tell me I am special and wanted and loved. That makes me so happy!

I lie back in Night's wise and gentle arms, snuggling under the covers where it's safe and soft and warm. I am not worried now. I know my Happy's home.

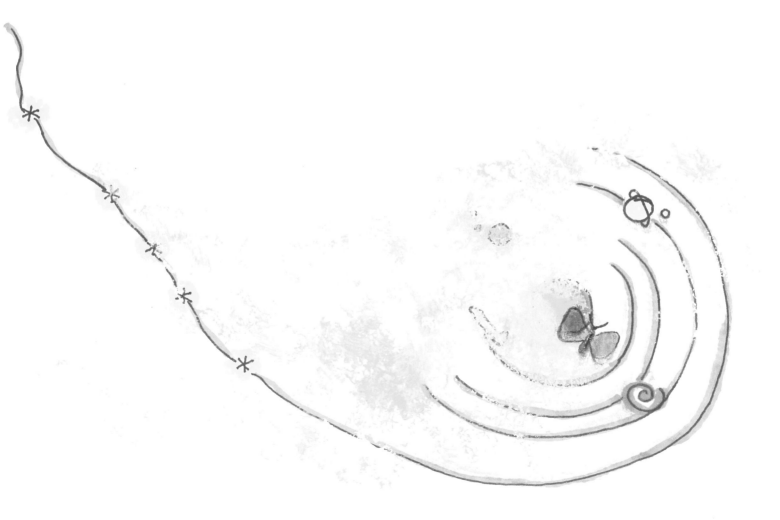

Happy, were you really gone? Or have you been here all along?

CPSIA information can be obtained
at www.ICGtesting.com
Printed in the USA
BVHW021317290719
554565BV00007B/80/P

* 9 7 8 1 7 9 6 0 4 6 8 4 7 *